JOY

Written by
YASMEEN ISMAIL

Illustrated by
JENNI DESMOND

WALKER BOOKS
AND SUBSIDIARIES
LONDON · BOSTON · SYDNEY · AUCKLAND

Oh boy! Oh boy!
My favourite toy.
I feel joy!

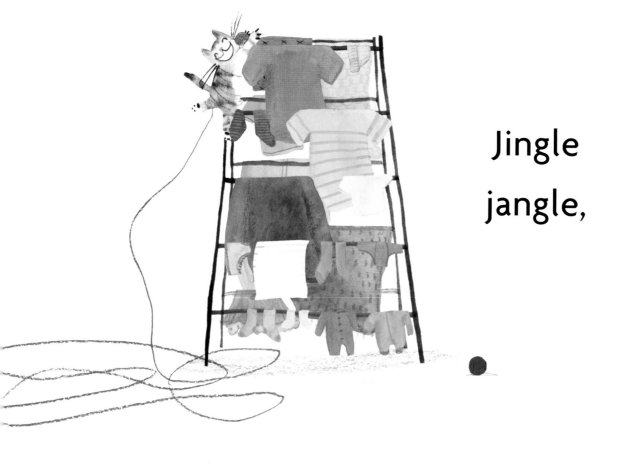

Jingle
jangle,

wriggle
wrangle,

in

a

tangle.

BOUNCE BOUNCE BOING BOING

Shake,
rattle
and

ROLL,

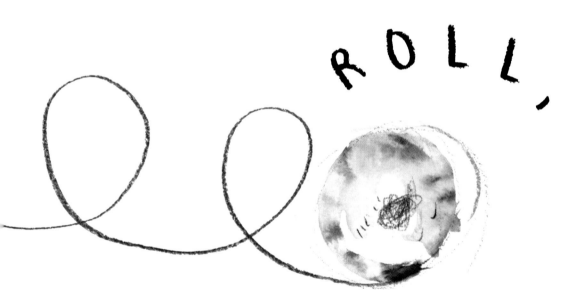

this happy soul!

Tickle, tickle,

in a pickle.

Run, run, fun, fun.

ZOOM-ZOOM   ZIM-ZAM

CLIP-CLOP   HIP-HOP

What a trip,
don't stop!

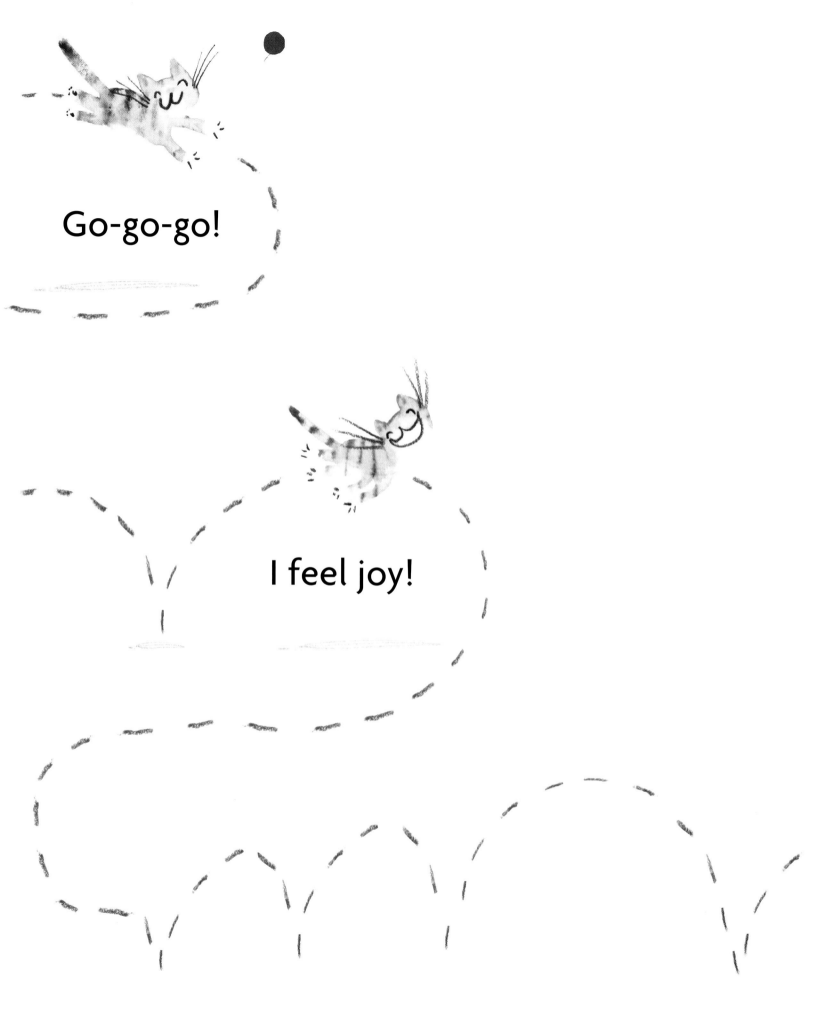

Go-go-go!

I feel joy!

UH-OH.

DONK   Ow.

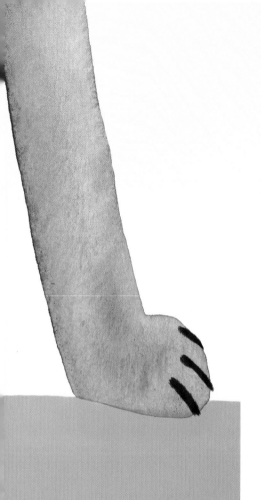

Oh...
This is bad.
I feel sad.

Where's my mum?
Where's my dad?

A little hug, a kiss, a squeeze,
let's check your paws,
and clean your knees.

I think you're going to be just fine.
Give yourself a little time.

Now look at me, are you all right?
Did you get a little fright?

I'm always here if you fall.

All you have to do is call.

There's nowhere that
I'd rather be,
than holding you
so close to me.

Oh boy!

Oh boy!

My favourite toy.

I feel joy!